ROCKS

PRAISE FOR THE MS WIZ BOOKS:

"Funny, magical . . . with wicked pictures
by Tony Ross, it's the closest thing you'll
get to Roald Dahl"
The Times

"Wonderfully funny and exciting"
Books for Keeps

"Ms Wiz is everyone's favourite"
Young Calibre Library

"Hilarious and hysterical"
Sunday Times

"The fantastic Ms Wiz books"
Malorie Blackman

TERENCE BLACKER

Ms Wiz

ROCKS

Illustrated by
TONY ROSS

ANDERSEN PRESS
LONDON

First published in Great Britain in 2009
by Andersen Press Limited
20 Vauxhall Bridge Road
London SW1V 2SA
www.andersenpress.co.uk

2 3 4 5 6 7 8 9 10

You're Nicked, Ms Wiz first published in 1989 by Piccadilly Press Limited

British Library Cataloguing in Publication Data available.

ISBN 978 184 270 848 4

Printed and bound in Great Britain by Clays Ltd, Elcograf S.p.A.

Ms Wiz

Ms Wiz

ROCKS

CHAPTER ONE
A FEW OOMPAHS
NEVER HURT ANYONE

A very strange noise was in the air. Sometimes it sounded like a racing car going round a bend.

"Beeeeeaaaaeeeooooouuuu . . ."

Then, quite without warning, the noise would toot and trumpet like an elephant losing its temper.

"Toooot . . . trumptrumptrump . . . Toootooooot."

There would be moments when an old steam engine seemed to have arrived in the town.

"Chuhhachuhhauchuhhachuff."

Occasionally, there would be a series of quieter sounds like those rude noises your grandfather makes after eating too much Sunday dinner.

"Pht . . . pht . . . phwwwwwt."

1

And then suddenly the racing car, the elephant, the steam engine and your grandfather would return – together.

"Beeeaaaa . . . trumptrump . . . chuhhachuff . . . pht."

The noise seemed to be loudest around Rylett Road. There the birds had flown out of the trees in alarm and parents brought their children in from the garden and rang one another to find out what was going on.

"Is it an animal?" asked Mrs Jones. "It sounds like it might be in pain."

"Maybe it's a new kind of burglar alarm," said Mr Edberg. "It would certainly scare me away."

All the neighbours agreed. Something had to be done about the strange and terrible noise.

At 15 Rylett Road, Cuthbert Harris, father of Peter (who was known to all his friends as "Podge") sat in his favourite armchair, reading the paper.

"The lad's music lesson's going well, Mother," he said loudly to his wife Mary, who sat opposite him.

"Half past five," said Mrs Harris.

"Me too," said Mr Harris. He patted both ears. "And buying these earplugs for us both was an excellent idea of mine. We can't hear a thing."

Mrs Harris nodded. "Chicken pie and beans," she said.

Just then, a man with long white hair and wild staring eyes tottered unsteadily into the room.

"C-c-can't take it any more," he muttered.

Mr Harris took out his earplugs. "Finished Peter's lesson already, Mr Jericho?" he asked. "My, doesn't time fly when there's lovely music in the air?"

"Lovely music? *Lovely*?" Mr Jericho, the music teacher, put his hands to his head. "That son of yours is playing notes that have never been invented."

"Oh yes, he's talented all right." Mr Harris chuckled. "I knew the trombone would be his instrument. I do love a brass band. It's the oompahs that get me every time."

"We'll see you next Tuesday then, Mr Jericho," said Mrs Harris, taking out her earplugs.

"I don't think you will," said Mr Jericho. "Peter's a nice enough lad but, between you and me, he hasn't got a musical bone in that rather large body of his. Maybe you could encourage him

4

to do something quieter – read books, or go for walks. Very long walks, if possible."

"Now, Mr Jericho—"

But before Mr Harris could finish his sentence, the music teacher was backing towards the door. "Don't bother to pay me," he said with a little wave of his hand. "My freedom from this house will be reward enough."

And he was gone.

"How very strange," said Mrs Harris.

"No backbone, these musicians." Mr Harris sniffed contemptuously. "I bet he plays the violin."

"Maybe you should have let Peter play the guitar," said Mrs Harris nervously. "That was what he had his heart set on."

"Guitar?" Cuthbert Harris shuddered with disgust. "And we all know where that leads. Long hair and inappropriate behaviour, that's where. No, a brass band is what I like. It's the sound of life, of progress. A manly sound. You can't go wrong in this world when you play the trombone, that's what I always say."

The doorbell rang.

"That'll be Mr Jericho," said Mr Harris. "I knew he'd change his mind."

But when Mrs Harris opened the front door, it was her neighbours Mrs Jones and Mr Edberg who were there.

"We're collecting names for a petition," said Mrs Jones. "It's about this terrible noise we've been hearing. We want the police to investigate."

"Noise? Police?" said Mrs Harris faintly.

"Will you sign the petition, Mary?" asked Mr Edberg. "Everyone else in the street has."

Glancing nervously over her shoulder, Mrs Harris signed.

When she returned to the sitting room, she sat down thoughtfully.

"Cuthbert, there's a bit of a problem with Peter and his trombone," she said. "There's a petition about it."

"Petition?" said Mr Harris.

"By the neighbours," said Mrs Harris. "About the noise."

"Stuff and nonsense," said Mr Harris. "A few oompahs never hurt anyone."

"They mentioned the police."

Mr Harris sighed. "I'll talk to the lad," he said.

"Now don't hurt his feelings, Cuthbert," said Mrs Harris. "You know how sensitive he can be."

"Trust me," said Mr Harris. "I'm a dad."

*

A few moments later, Mr Harris stood in the middle of Podge's room.

"There's a problem with that trombone, son," he said. "The problem is that you're completely useless at playing it."

Podge looked up from the bed. "But—"

"Mr Jericho says you haven't got a musical bone in your body. The neighbours are revolting, too. They've said that if you blow into that thing once more" – he nodded in the direction of the trombone on Podge's bed – "it'll be a matter for the police."

"I like music," said Podge quietly.

"The problem is music doesn't like you," said his father. He picked up the trombone. "I'll look after that. It's caused quite enough trouble already."

With the trombone under his arm, Mr Harris left the room, closing the door firmly behind him.

He stood on the landing outside, and smiled. Yes. He thought he had handled that rather well.

Alone and trombone-less, Podge reached for his mobile phone and rang his best friend Jack Beddows.

"Hey," he said.

"Hey," said Jack.

"Kickabout?" said Podge.

"Cool," said Jack.

Five minutes later, in the local park, Podge stood watching Jack bouncing a football on his foot.

"I suppose I should have guessed there was a problem with my music when my parents bought earplugs," he said.

"It's not a great sign," Jack agreed. "I wanted my mum to buy me a drum set. 'She said I had to practise first. 'Practise?' I said. 'Er, on what exactly?' 'The table,' she said. 'The table!'"

Jack booted the football high in the air. It came to rest in some bushes near the entrance to the park. As they walked towards it, Podge and Jack heard the sound of music. They crouched in the bushes and peered through the railings.

On the pavement across the street, a woman was standing in front of an upturned hat. She was playing what looked like a very small guitar.

Although she was dressed rather oddly – a battered straw hat, dark glasses and ripped three-quarter length jeans – there was something familiar about the black nail varnish on her fingernails.

Jack and Podge looked at one another as the same thought occurred to both of them.

Ms Wiz? Playing music?

CHAPTER TWO
GROOVE WITH THE MAGIC

Actually, Ms Wiz was not bad at playing music. But she wasn't great either.

Podge and Jack crossed the road and listened politely as, with a slightly mad smile on her face, she sang her song.

"Take time to smell the flowers
See the birdies in the sky
Let's run barefoot when it showers
Wave our arms like a butterfly."

She stopped playing but, just as Podge and Jack clapped their hands, she started singing again – more loudly this time.

"Wave your arms like a butterfly!
Like a lovely, groovy bu-tter-flyyyyy."

"Whoa," said Jack, now that she really did seem to have finished. "Cool song, Ms Wiz."

"D'you like it?" said Ms Wiz. "I wrote it in 1967."

"1967?" said Podge. "But that's years ago."

"The summer of love, it was called, because love was all around us. You could feel it in your fingers and feel it in your toes."

"How old were you then?" asked Jack. "I mean, if you were about twenty then, that means that now you're—"

"Forever young," said Ms Wiz quickly. "Back in 1967, everybody thought they were forever young. But I think I'm right in saying I'm the only person who has actually managed it."

She reached into the bag that was beside her on the pavement and took out a pair of drumsticks, which she handed to Jack. Then she took out a small instrument like the one she had been playing and gave it to Podge.

"This is called a ukulele," she said. "All the best guitarists start on a uke." She looked at them both. "Maybe we could play together."

Podge winced. "There's a bit of a problem with music and me," he said. "My teacher Mr Jericho says—" He stopped. There was a faint humming sound in the air.

"I know that sound," said Jack. "It means that magic's about to happen."

Ms Wiz shook her head. "It's just

giving me the note. We're doing this one in the key of C. One, two, three, four—"

She started to play her ukulele.

"Take time to smell the flowers . . ."

Jack glanced at Podge, and shrugged. He began to tap his drumsticks in time on the railing. Suddenly, as if his hands no longer belonged to him, he was drumming out a fast beat.

Podge held the ukulele in front of him. His fingers came to life and strummed the strings.

"What's happening?" he said as music poured out of the uke.

". . . wave our arms like a butterfly," sang Ms Wiz.

The music that Podge and Jack were playing was faster than Ms Wiz's tune, so that it began to seem as if she were in the background.

Suddenly, without even knowing he was doing it, Podge began to sing.

"Sixty-seven?
They thought it was heaven
They were forever young
They once were freaky
But now they're creaky
So let's show them how it's done."

Jack laughed, as he did a little roll of rhythm with his drumsticks.
Podge pointed at Ms Wiz.

"You say she's a hippy
But I don't buy it
That peace and love —
Why don't we try it?

"Birdies and butterflies
Are not so tragic
Let's get on down
And groove with the magic."

Now Jack joined in with the chorus.

"The summer of love is back
The summer of love is back
Listen to the Wiz
Look out, she's the biz
The summer of love is back."

Ms Wiz closed her eyes and swayed
to her own music.

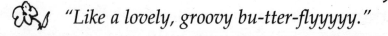

"Like a lovely, groovy bu-tter-flyyyyy."

By now a crowd of children with their parents had gathered around. As Ms Wiz, Podge and Jack played, there were murmurs of admiration. When they finished, everyone started clapping.

"That was amazing," said a young mother, standing at the front of the crowd with a pram. "It was a crazy fusion thing – a bit of hip-hop, a bit of grandparent hippy music from the Sixties."

"Hey, we've invented hippy-hop," said Jack.

But Ms Wiz was frowning. "Did you say "grandparent music"?" she asked.

The woman shrugged. "Well, it is from quite a long time ago," she said.

"We're talking about our generation," said Ms Wiz. "All we are saying is give peace a chance. What's so funny about peace, love and understanding?"

"Those kids are amazing," said a

man Podge recognised as living in his street. "How did you learn to play like that, Peter?"

Podge glanced nervously at Jack. "It just sort of came naturally," he said.

"Yeah," said Jack. "As if by magic."

"What's the name of your group?" a little girl asked shyly.

There was a moment's silence. Then Ms Wiz stepped forward. "We call ourselves The Groovy Butterflies of Universal Peace and Love."

"We do?" said Jack.

"Great name, Ms Wiz," muttered Podge. "Really snappy."

"Perhaps we could shorten it to the first letters of the name," said Jack. "That would be" – it took a moment for him to work it out – "GBOUPAL."

"You should put your stuff on the internet," said the woman with the pram. "Have you tried MySpace?"

"We're quite happy with our own

space, thank you very much," said Ms Wiz.

The woman looked confused. "What about Facebook?"

"I don't wear make-up," said Ms Wiz. She took the ukulele from Podge and the drumsticks from Jack, and then turned to the crowd. "Thank for listening to the Groovy Butterflies of Universal Peace and Love."

With that she picked up her bag and began walking down the street. Smiling apologetically to the crowd, Podge and Jack followed her.

"Is that it, Ms Wiz? Aren't we going to play again?" asked Podge as he tried to keep up with her."

"It's always best to keep the audience wanting more," said Ms Wiz.

"But we could be pop stars," said Jack. "In a couple of months, the name of our group could be on everyone's lips – GBOUPAL."

"I don't want to be a pop star," said Ms Wiz. "Fame isn't all it's made out to be."

At that moment, Ms Wiz and Jack noticed that Podge had stopped walking. They walked back to where he was standing. He was staring back to where they had been playing. "All I wanted to do was play some more songs. I was living my dream back there."

Ms Wiz seemed to think for a moment. "I'll be playing outside the park tomorrow at the same time. Now I'd better be off."

She took out her mobile and began to dial. As they watched, she faded slowly from view.

"Did all that actually happen?" Jack murmured to Podge.

Podge was clicking his fingers in time to a beat in his head. "The summer of love is back," he said. "Oh yeah, the summer of love is back."

CHAPTER THREE
I'M TALENTED, MAKE ME A STAR!

Later that evening, as usual, the Harris family sat down to watch their favourite TV programme *The Avenue*. The previous night on *The Avenue*, Doreen, who lived at number 23, had been seen kissing Phil, the new landlord at the Crown, and the Avenue's local gossip Jason (who has just moved into number six) had told Doreen's husband Ashok.

"This is really great." Mr Harris rubbed his hands as the opening credits rolled. "I can't imagine what life would be like without *The Avenue*."

"Ssshh," said Mrs Harris, nodding in the direction of Podge. "The boy's trying to listen."

But, although Podge was staring at the screen, his thoughts were not on *The*

Avenue at all but on what it had been like to play the ukulele and to sing in time with his strumming fingers.

Just then, the telephone rang.

"Oh, bother," said Mr Harris. "Who can that be? Everyone knows we have family time in front of the telly after we've had our tea."

"Let's leave it, Dad," said Mrs Harris.

The telephone kept ringing.

"I'll get it," said Podge, standing up. "It could be Jack."

He walked into the hall and picked up the receiver.

"Oh, hiiiii there." The man's voice on the other end of the telephone sounded odd, as if he was talking while trying to smile at the same time. "Is that the Harris household?"

"Yes," said Podge.

"Could I speak to the musician in the family?"

Podge frowned. "I think you might

have got a wrong number," he said.

"It's Peter Harris I'm looking for," said the man. "Plays the ukulele and sings like an angel, I've been told. Would that be you by any chance?"

"I'm not exactly musical," said Podge."

"Hr-hr-hr-hr-hr." The man's laughter sounded like someone trying to start a car with a rather flat battery. "And he's modest, too. I like that in my young stars."

"Who is this?" asked Podge.

"I am Cy," said the man. "Cy Smoothe. You might have seen me on one of my shows – *Have I Really Got Talent?*, or *Crazy But Talented*, or *Talent Swap* or even *The World's Most Incredibly Talented Celebrities*."

"Cy Smoothe," said Podge. "Are you the judge who's always very rude?

"That's me, hr-hr-hr," said Cy Smoothe. "I'm famous for my catchphrases – 'That's appaaaaaalling!'

and 'That's amaaaaazing!'." He did
his dead-motor laugh again. "Now the
good news, Pete, is that we're looking
for acts for our new show. You'll never
guess the title."

"I dunno. Maybe something to do
with talent?"

"Brilliant! You must be psychic, Pete.
It's called *I'm Talented, Make Me a Star!*
And, Pete, one of my team happens to
live in your road and he caught you and
your friends busking in the park this
afternoon. And we want your group,
the" – Podge heard the sound of rustling
paper – "ah yes, the Groovy Butterflies
of Universal Peace and Love, to appear
on our first show. The word on the street
is that you could be the next big thing."

"But we don't—"

"Great, great. Here's the address and
my mobile number. Tomorrow at five."

Podge noted the details on a pad
beside the telephone.

"Now, Pete love, you will there, won't you?" asked Cy Smoothe.

"Ummmm . . . well—" said Podge.

"That's perfect. In fact . . . That's amaaaaazing! Byee."

Podge wandered back into the sitting room. His parents were staring at the screen. Mrs Harris seemed to be crying.

"You missed Ashok's row with Doreen," she said. "It was heartbreaking."

"Serves her right," said Mr Harris. "That Doreen's no better than she should be."

"That was Cy Smoothe, the famous TV celebrity, on the telephone," said Podge. "He wants me to appear in a national talent show."

"Very nice, dear," said Mrs Harris, her eyes still fixed to the screen. "Now come and watch *The Avenue*."

"Uh-oh," said Podge's father. "Phil's come to see Doreen to find out what's happened. Now there'll be trouble."

At first, when Jack met Podge in the park the next day, he refused to believe what Podge was saying.

"Cy Smoothe called you? Personally? He wants us to play on his show?"

Podge nodded. "Yup."

"That's . . . that's amaaaaazing!" Jack did a little dance. "I'm going to be a star, I'm going to be star," he sang.

"Yeah, yeah," said Podge. "But you seem to have forgotten one small problem. We can't actually play any music."

"With a bit of magic, we can," laughed Jack. "Let's go and see Ms Wiz. She'll be up for it."

Ms Wiz was standing in the same place, with the same hat in front of her, singing the same song.

*"Wave your wings like a butterfly!
Like a lovely, groovy bu-tter-flyyyyy."*

When she finished, Podge and Jack clapped politely.

"It's very good," Podge said politely. "But do you know any other songs?"

"Of course I do," said Ms Wiz. "Here's another of my favourite number from the 1960s." She strummed her ukulele. "I just hope I can remember the words." She took a deep breath.

*"Ting-a-ling
Ting-a-ling,
I'm just sitting here
Doing my thing . . ."*

"Oh dear," murmured Jack.
Ms Wiz glanced at him, then
strummed her ukulele once more.

*"Hear me sing
In the spring
Look at me
I really . . . I really . . ."*

"Ming?" suggested Jack.
"What does that mean?" asked Ms
Wiz.
"It's a modern word for being
groovy." Podge nudged Jack hard in the
ribs.
"Hey!" Ms Wiz punched the air. "I
ming!"
"Ms Wiz, we need to talk to you

about Cy Smoothe," said Podge. "He called me last night."

"Smoothe. What a very odd name," said Ms Wiz. "Who is he?"

"You must have heard of Cy Smoothe," said Jack. "He's big on TV."

"I don't care where he's big. And I'm not interested in TV."

"Does that mean you won't want our group to be on his talent show?" asked Jack.

"Our group?" Ms Wiz plucked thoughtfully at a string on her ukulele. "You mean he's into our sounds, man?"

"He certainly is," said Podge. "He thinks the Groovy Butterflies of Universal Peace and Love could be the next big thing."

"The next big thing. I've always wanted to be the next big thing." Ms Wiz smiled. "I rather like the sound of Mr Smoothe," she said.

"The only trouble is that he wants us

to audition for his show and the audition starts in about half an hour's time."

"And it's on the other side of town," said Jack.

"And we haven't enough money for a taxi." He looked into the hat which Ms Wiz had left on the pavement. It contained one 20p coin. "Nor have you."

"Do you have Mr Smoothe's telephone number?" asked Ms Wiz.

Podge reached into the pocket of his trousers and took out a piece of paper. "Here's the number he gave me," he said, passing it to Ms Wiz.

She took a small, bright pink mobile phone from her bag and began to dial the number.

"There's no point in talking to him," said Jack. "He's just about to do a show. What's that noise?"

All around them, a low humming

sound could be heard.

"Place one finger each on the phone, boys," said Ms Wiz. "This is a real mobile. It can move us to the exact place of the phone whose number I've dialled."

The humming sound grew louder.

Nervously, Podge and Jack extended a finger and touched the phone. Immediately they felt a tingling in their feet, which rose slowly up their legs. Jack glanced down and made an odd gulping noise.

"Don't look now, Podge," he said. "But I think we're vanishing."

"Hang on, Ms Wiz!" There was panic in Podge's voice. "What about my— "

But by the time he had finished the sentence, all three of them, with the ukulele and the bag and the hat, had disappeared. Podge's last word hung in the air above an empty street.

"—tea?"

CHAPTER FOUR
YOU GOTTA DAZZLE, KID

"And *who* are you?"

Those were the first words that Jack and Podge heard after their journey through space. There had been a roaring in their ears, a sense that their bodies had been travelling through the air at the speed of a bullet, a firework display of lights in front of their closed eyes, and then –

"I said, who are *you*? And, come to think of it, why are you standing around my desk in my office with your fingers on my mobile telephone?"

Podge slowly opened his eyes. They were in an office. The man who had been talking was small, dark-haired and reminded Podge of someone he knew. His finger was touching an elegant grey phone which lay on a desk.

Beside him, Ms Wiz seemed to stir into life, removing her finger from the phone and rubbing it against her other hand. "It's just a magic thing," she explained. "We happen to be able to travel through space at the speed of a text message. It's nothing special."

The dark-haired man frowned and turned to a young woman who stood nearby, holding a clipboard. "Who are these people, Trudi?" he murmured. "And what are they doing in my office?"

"Search me, Cy," said the woman called Trudi. "I'll call security to get them thrown out."

"Cy!" Podge spoke the name out loud. Now he knew who the man had reminded of. He looked like a smaller, older, crosser version of Cy Smoothe when he was on TV.

"Have we met?" The man narrowed his eyes suspiciously. "Or are you just a fan?"

"We spoke on the phone today," said Podge. "I'm Peter Harris. You said that our group The Groovy Butterflies of Universal Peace and Love were going to be the next big thing."

Cy gave a little laugh. "Well, I can see that you're certainly going to be the next big thing. In fact, you're quite a big thing already."

Embarrassed, Podge put his hands in front of his stomach.

Trudi whispered in Cy Smoothe's ear.

He listened to her, nodding slowly. When he turned back to Podge, Jack and Ms Wiz, a wide smile was in place. "Ah, yes. *Those* Groovy Butterflies of Universal Peace and Love," he said, extending a hand to Podge. "How could it have slipped my mind?"

Podge shook his hand. "And this is Jack," he said.

"Yo, Jack." Cy Smoothe held up a hand. "Gimme five." With a little wince, Jack slapped his hand.

"And this is Ms Wiz," said Podge.

Cy winked at Ms Wiz. "Hi, Mum. Glad you could come along," he said.

Ms Wiz gave a little start, as if someone had just squirted water in her face.

"Excuse me," she said. "I am not anyone's mum."

"Yeah yeah, manager, whatevs," said Cy Smoothe.

"As it happens," said Ms Wiz with a

proud little smile. "I was told only yesterday that I ming."

"Actually," said Jack quickly. "It was Ms Wiz who—"

"Hey, kids." Cy Smoothe held up a hand. "I could stand around shooting the breeze with you all day but, bottom line, I've got a hit TV show to produce in" – he glanced at a large watch on his wrist – "seven minutes' time."

"And what do we have to do for the audition?" asked Podge.

"Do?" Cy Smoothe glanced at his assistant Trudi. "The kid needs to know what he has to do, hr-hr-hr." Suddenly the smile on his face was gone. "You gotta dazzle, kid. You gotta shine. You gotta knock my socks off with your incredible star quality. *Comprende?*"

Without another word, he left the office.

"Sorry about that," said Trudi. "We've had a bad day. The guy who was going to play *Moon River* on the musical handsaw had an accident and cut his finger. It was so sad – we really needed that saw player. Shall I show you to the rehearsal room?"

The rehearsal room was not a room at all. It was a big, brightly lit hall, packed with adults and children and animals and music and noise. In every corner of the room, there was someone practising for the big moment when they hoped Cy Smoothe would make them a star.

"Who are all these people?" Ms Wiz covered her ears with her hands. "I really don't like crowds."

"We put an advertisement in the newspaper, asking for anyone with talent to come for auditions for the show," said Trudi.

"But" – Jack watched a rather large man who had been juggling three

oranges drop them one after the other –
"they haven't got talent."

"You know that. I know that. Anyone
with eyes and ears would know that.
But they don't."

A man with spiky hair and comedy
glasses walked up to them, waving a
pack of cards like fan. "Take a card, any
card," he said to Ms Wiz.

"Not now, sonny," said Ms Wiz.

"Don't you like magic, then?" the
man asked, winking at Ms Wiz.

"Uh-oh," said Jack.

"I'm not in the mood," said Ms Wiz
coldly.

"Ooooh, get her," said the magician
to Podge. "She's too posh for magic."

Sighing, Ms Wiz turned to him. "Oh,
if you insist," she said, clicking her
fingers in the direction of the cards. All
the symbols slid off the cards and fell to
the ground. Running through the clubs,
hearts, spades and diamonds on the

floor were the brightly dressed figures of kings, queens and jacks. Two jokers were chasing one another.

"They're the characters you see on cards," laughed Podge. "They've come to life."

"Hey, that's good." The magician shook his head in admiration. "That's really good. Are you in the business?"

"I *am* the business," said Ms Wiz.

A tiny king and queen were wandering off, hand in hand.

"Could you put them back on the cards now?" asked the magician. "I don't want to lose them."

But Ms Wiz had turned to Trudi. "Now we'll just need a small table on stage," she said. "It's for Jack to play his drumsticks on."

"Please, miss. *Please*. I'm losing my kings and queens," said the magician.

Ms Wiz clicked her fingers and the figures and symbols were back on the cards. "Magic should never be used for personal gain," she said. "It's one of my golden rules."

Podge was looking around him. "We're going to be here all night," he murmured to Jack. "What about my tea?"

Trudi glanced around her. Dropping her voice, she said, "We'll hear you early. The fact is we know who's going to get through the audition already."

"You do?" said Jack.

"We'll have a girl group called The Hey Babes." She pointed to two dark-haired girls and a blonde who were standing moodily in one corner. There's a young comedian called Darren Quip, a grandpa who plays old songs on a piano, a five-year-old girl singer called Millie Piper the Little Nightingale with a gap in her front teeth and a woman called Frieda with her dog Billy who sings hits from the 1980s. They call their act Absolutely Barking." She glanced at her watch. "You should be on soon," she said.

Ms Wiz was shaking her head. "A singing dog?" she said. "Did you just say we're competing with a singing dog?"

Before Trudi could reply, a voice was heard over the loudspeaker system. "Cy Smoothe is ready for the first acts. Could we please have The Groovy Butterflies of Universal Peace and Love on stage, please?"

The next five minutes were like the strangest of dreams. Podge, Jack and Ms Wiz followed Trudi to a door which led to the place where the audition would take place. They walked down some steps, along a twisting corridor, through a curtain and on to the stage, which was completely dark, except for one spotlight which lit up a small table.

"The table's for Jack to drum on," Trudi whispered. "Cy will guide you through."

Nervously they moved into the centre of the stage. The brightness of the light made their eyes ache.

"OK, Butterflies." The voice of Cy Smoothe came at them out of the darkness. "What will you be playing for us tonight?"

"We shall be playing one of our own compositions," said Ms Wiz. "It is called *Take Time to Smell the—*"

"*The Summer of Love is Back*," said Podge quickly.

"I prefer *Take Time to Smell the Flowers*," said Ms Wiz. "It's really important in this life that, when everyone's so busy, they should just remember the beauty of the lovely little flowers."

"Never mind the lovely little flowers," Cy Smoothe shouted. "Just get on with the song."

Ms Wiz reached into her bag and took out two ukuleles and a pair of drumsticks. She handed Podge and Jack their instruments, a low humming noise could be heard around them – and suddenly they were playing the music again.

The song seemed to be over in no time. When they finished, there was a brief moment of silence, followed by a murmur of voices from the darkness.

"OK." It was Cy Smoothe again.

"You're in the final of *I've Got Talent, Make Me a Star!* Trudi will give you the details."

"Yeah!" said Podge and Jack together.

"You were great, boys," said Cy from the darkness.

Ms Wiz cleared her throat. "Ahem," she said. "Boys?"

"Sorry, love. The backing track was fine, too. Really funny."

Trudi appeared on the stage with the next act, The Hey Babes. "Can you find your way back to the rehearsal room?" she asked Ms Wiz.

As they walked down the corridor, Ms Wiz muttered to herself. "Backing track? Funny? What did he mean?"

"I really think we should get back," said Podge.

"Quite right," said Ms Wiz, taking out her pink mobile phone. "We've had enough fun for one night. It's time to vanish. Fingers on the phone!"

*

Slowly Podge opened his eyes. He was in the park.

"Was that a dream?" said Jack, who was standing beside him.

Ms Wiz tapped her pink phone. "It's a marvellous little mobile, this one. I just press "Redial" and it takes me back to where I was when I made my last call. I think everyone should have one."

"Which means we've just been talking to Cy Smoothe and he's going to make us famous in a week's time," said Jack

"Fame isn't all it's cracked up to be," said Ms Wiz. "Your life is no longer your own. Everyone wants a part of you. Photographers camp outside your doorstep. You can't even go shopping without complete strangers asking for your autograph."

"Oh no," said Jack. "And my writing's terrible. I'd better start practising my autograph right now."

"Hang on." Podge closed his eyes, as if trying to work out a particularly difficult thought. "You said that magic should never be used for selfish purposes," he said to Ms Wiz.

"It's my golden rule," said Ms Wiz.

"So what are we doing with our music spell? We'd be winning a talent competition when we haven't really got any talent."

"Speak for yourself," said Jack.

"It just seems a bit unfair on the rest," said Podge.

"That's showbiz," said Jack. "It's dog eat dog out there – or dog eat singing dog in our case."

Ms Wiz reached into her case and took out a ukulele which she handed to Podge. "You're absolutely right," she said. "If we're going to appear on television next week, we had all better start practising."

Podge plucked at a string. It made sad, tuneless note. "On the other hand, maybe a bit of magic wouldn't hurt."

"No," said Ms Wiz firmly. "If the Groovy Butterflies of Universal Peace and Love can't play without magic, then we don't deserve to win anything. We should do it for real or not at all."

She took out a book from her bag. "This shows you how to play the ukulele. We'll meet every day in the park to have a practice."

She began to dial on her mobile phone. "Same place, same time tomorrow?" she said as she began to vanish.

Before Podge or Jack could reply, she was gone.

"Nice one, Podge," said Jack. "Now what are we going to do?"

Podge strummed the ukulele. It made a tuneless, jangling sound. "Panic," he said.

CHAPTER FIVE
A WITCH WITH A GUITAR

Mr Harris was not pleased when his son returned from the park with a new musical instrument.

"You know what I've always told you, Peter Harris," he said. "There'll be no guitars in this house. Guitars only lead to unnecessariness."

"It's not a guitar," said Podge. "It's called a ukulele."

Mrs Harris walked in from the kitchen. "A ukulele?" she said. "Oh I do love the sound of a ukulele. It reminds me of the music my parents used to play when I was young. Can you play *Tiptoe Through The Tulips*?"

"Er— "

"See what I mean?" snapped Mr Harris. "Your mother's gone

unnecessary already. Where did you get that thing anyway?"

Podge winced. It was the question he had been dreading. "Jack and I happened to meet an old friend in the park. She just happened to be playing some music and happened to have some spare instruments with her."

"That's nice, Peter," said his mother. "What's your friend's name?"

Podge took a deep breath. "Ms Wiz," he mumbled hurriedly. "Now I think I'll go to my room and practise."

"Hang on," said Mr Harris. "Did you just say Wiz? You are not, I very much hope, referring to that witch woman who turns teachers into geese and policemen into rabbits."

"Paranormal Operative, Cuthbert," said Mrs Harris. "Ms Wiz says that calling her a witch gives people the wrong idea."

"I speak as I find," said Mr Harris.

'A witch is a witch is a witch. And if there's one thing worse than a witch, it's a witch with a guitar."

"Ukulele," said Podge and Mrs Harris together.

"She spells trouble, that woman. I'll not have my family messing around with magic, and that's final."

"We formed a group – Jack, Ms Wiz and me," said Podge quietly. "We were going to be on a TV talent show next week."

"Talent show?" Mr Harris laughed. "Don't talk daft. The only talent you've got is for eating pies."

"That was what the telephone call last night was about," said Podge. "It was Cy Smoothe, asking us to audition for his new show *I'm Talented, Make Me a Star!* It starts next week."

"D'you mean Cy 'That's appaaaalling' Smoothe?" said Mrs Harris. "I like him."

"Stuff and nonsense." Mr Harris reached for a TV guide. "What's your group called anyway?"

"The Groovy Butterflies of Universal Peace and Love," said Podge.

"Lovely name," said Mrs Harris.

"Groovy butterflies?" muttered Mr Harris. "Groovy troublemakers, more like it. Oh—" Something in the TV Guide seemed to have caught his eye. "As it happens there is a new Cy Smoothe series. And it is called *I'm Talented, Make Me a Star!* You've been looking through this guide, haven't you, Peter? I've told you about telling—"

"He can't have, Cuthbert," Mrs Harris interrupted. "We bought it while he was in the park."

Mr Harris was staring at the guide in his hands. "It says here that's there's a prize of £100,000 for the winner of the show," he said faintly.

"We're not really in it for the money," said Podge.

"One hundred thousand big ones." A strange smile had settled on Mr Harris's face. "Maybe I was a little hasty about the unnecessariness."

Podge frowned. "You mean— ?"

"I'll tell you what I mean, son," said Mr Harris. "I mean get practising – now!"

Alone in his room, Podge opened the book which Ms Wiz had given him. It was called *Learn the Ukulele in a Day*. He learned how to tune the ukulele, and where to put his fingers. He strummed nervously. Then he began to sing quietly.

Outside his bedroom door, Mr and Mrs Harris were listening.

"He's got a bit of a way to go before he can play for Cy Smoothe," said Mrs Harris.

"Stuff and nonsense," said Mr Harris. "I always said that boy had talent. £100,000. I could buy a new car. And golf clubs!"

At first, when Podge met Ms Wiz and Jack in the park to practise together without magic, the noise they made frightened the birds away. By the third day, they were more or less starting and finishing at the same time. By the fifth, people were gathering around to listen to them. When they sang The Summer of Love is Back, it sounded different from the way it had been when they were under the influence of magic but people still clapped in time to it and applauded when they finished playing. "I think," said Ms Wiz, smiling at Podge and Jack, "that the Groovy Butterflies of Universal Peace and Love are ready for the big time."

CHAPTER SIX
LOSE THE HIPPY

The day of the show began badly. Trudi, Cy Smoothe's assistant, rang Podge early that morning to tell them that a car would be collecting them at eleven o'clock.

"What clothes should we wear?" asked Podge.

"Just be natural," said Trudi. "Natural and smart."

That was where the trouble began.

"Smart?" said Mr Harris. "We'll put him in that nice suit we bought him for cousin Lily's wedding."

"I'm meant to be playing in a rock group," said Podge.

"You can wear a really colourful tie if you like," said Mr Harris. "I'm not having my son appearing on TV looking like a ragamuffin."

Unfortunately, when he arrived at the front door, Jack was dressed rather differently. He looked as if he had been in a fight. His jeans were torn. There was a hole in one of his trainers and his big toe was sticking through it. Under his coat he was wearing a baggy T-shirt with the words "IRON BUTTERFLY" on it. The word "IRON" had been crossed out with marker pen and replaced with "GROOVY'.

"When my mum was young, she was a fan of this band called Iron Butterfly," Jack explained. "She said she always knew that T-shirt would be useful one day."

"But we were meant to be smart," said Podge.

Mr and Mrs Harris appeared in the hallway behind Podge. To his surprise, they hardly looked at Jack but were staring down the road.

"What on earth is *that*?" said Mrs Harris.

It was Ms Wiz. She looked like a fairground fortune-teller from a very bad, very old film. There was a wispy purple scarf around her head and she wore a billowing green and purple patchwork dress. Various heavy metal ornaments hung around her neck, making a jangly noise as she walked. She was barefoot.

As she approached the Harris's front door, she held up both hands in a V-shaped peace sign.

"Hey, Butterflies," she said. "Are we ready to make sweet music?"

"I hope you're not planning to go on national TV looking like that," said Mr Harris. "You look like you're going to a fancy dress party."

Ms Wiz put her face close to Mr Harris's. "What's it like in Straight City, man? Can you see me through the bars of the prison of your mind? I'm just doing my thing, OK? Hangin' loose, yeah? Like, the summer of love is totally, totally back."

"The summer of nutters more like," said Mr Harris.

"Hey, you, get offa my cloud," said Ms Wiz.

"Maybe I could lend you something," said Mrs Harris. "I've got a very nice coat and skirt."

But it was too late. At that moment, a long white limousine eased its way into the street. The car pulled up in front of the Harris's house. A driver in a uniform stepped out. "Is this the right address for the Groovy Butterflies of Universal Peace and Love?" he asked.

At the Cy Smoothe Television Theatre, Podge, Jack and Ms Wiz met the other acts who were going to take part on the programme. The Hey Babes were there, and so was Darren Quip, the comedian and Harry Brown, the piano player. The girl singer with a gap in her teeth, Millie Piper the Little Nightingale, sat nervously with her mother. Billy of Absolutely Barking was being given treats in a corner.

At first, Trudi was worried that Podge, Jack and Ms Wiz were dressed rather differently from one another. "One of you looks like a businessman from the 1980s, the other like a heavy metal rocker from the 1970s."

"And I'm from the 1960s," said Ms Wiz. "We're like a musical history lesson."

"Hm. I guess," said Trudi uncertainly.

As the audience arrived at the theatre that afternoon, Trudi gathered the acts together in a back room.

"Just go out and enjoy yourselves," she said, a big smile on her face. "We're on live TV. So, if anything goes a bit wrong, keep going at all costs."

Billy from Absolutely Barking made an odd whining sound.

"Nice doggie." Millie Piper the Little Nightingale was about to pat the dog.

"Don't touch the dog!" screamed Frieda. "He's just had his hair done."

"Here's one, here's one," said Darren Quip, the comedian. "How do you find a dog that's lost in the woods? Put your ear next to a tree and listen for the bark. Bark, get it? On the tree. Woof woof?"

"Would you like me to play *How*

Much Is That Doggie in the Window? on the Wurlitzer?" asked Harry "Mr Piano" Brown.

"Thank you, thank you, save it for the show," Trudi called out. "Now, you know how it goes. After you have performed, the three judges – Danny Diva, the celebrity chef, the actress Lorraine Bustle and Cy Smoothe – will tell you exactly what they think of it."

"And what do we do?" asked one of The Hey Babes.

"You keep smiling," said Trudi. "So first on will be Harry "Mr Piano" Brown. All right?"

From backstage, Podge, Jack and Ms Wiz waited nervously as the other acts performed. Harry Brown was greeted with polite applause. The Hey Babes had the audience clapping along with them. Millie Piper the Little Nightingale sang her song squeakily to huge cheers. There was nervous laughter for Darren

Quip, followed by boos when none of the judges liked his act.

Then it was their turn. "Taking us back in time," said the announcer. "Please welcome The Groovy Butterflies of Universal Peace and Love."

They walked on to the stage and took their place, smiling into the dazzling lights. Standing between Jack and Podge, Ms Wiz began to play.

"Take time to smell the flowers
See the birdies in the sky . . ."

There was a ripple of uncertain
laughter from the audience. Sitting
with the two other judges, Cy Smoothe
winced.

Then Podge began to strum. There
were only three chords in the song but,
even without the help of the magic,
he got the rhythm. Then Jack came in,
tapping out the rhythm on the table.

Soon the audience was clapping
along. By the time they hit the final
chorus, Podge felt himself smiling.

"The summer of love is back
The summer of love is back
Listen to the Wiz
Look out, she's the biz
The summer of love is back."

There was a crash of applause and
cheering as they hit the final note.
Slowly it died as the lights came up on
the three judges.

Danny Diva was writing on a pad in front of him. He looked up as if, just for a moment, he had forgotten he was on television.

"I like the look," he said. "And the name is hilarious. I like the boys dressed as a businessman and a heavy rocker. The comedian with flowers in her hair is kind of funny, too. You know what? I think you could go far in this competition."

"Comedian?" said Ms Wiz. "Who's the comedian?"

"Just keep smiling," Podge muttered.

Lorraine Bustle seemed to be in tears. "That was just so great," she said, dabbing at her eyes. "You've got youth. You've got age. Peter, you've got the most lovely voice I've ever heard. You've got everything. You're just . . . groovy!"

"Age? Who's got age?" said Ms Wiz, rather more loudly this time.

"*Keep smiling*," said Jack.

All eyes turned to Cy Smoothe.

"Boys," he said. "I have two words to say to you. That's amaaaazing!"

The audience erupted with applause.

"But—" He held up a hand for silence. "I've got to give you some tough advice, guys. You two are great but, if you're going to get on in this business, I have an important message for you." He paused, then pointed at Ms Wiz. "Lose the hippy," he said. "She's funny, in a weird sort of way, but frankly she's holding you back from stardom. She's *way* too old-fashioned."

"Hippy?" Ms Wiz took a step forward. "Funny? Way too old-fashioned?"

Cy Smoothe turned to the audience. "What does everyone else think?" he asked.

"Lose the hippy!" a woman shouted from the front row.

"Go home, love," said someone else. "Leave it to the kids."

"Excuse me—" Ms Wiz tried to speak but now the audience was chanting, "Lose the hippy! Lose the hippy! Lose the hippy!"

A low angry growl, which only Podge and Jack could hear, came from Ms Wiz, followed by a distant humming noise. "No magic, Ms Wiz" said Podge. "We agreed—"

The ukulele in Ms Wiz's hands seemed to be growing. Within seconds, it was a bright, gleaming electric guitar. Amazed, the audience fell silent.

Ms Wiz raised her hand high in the air, then brought it crashing down on the guitar where her fingers raced across the fretboard, making a deafening noise.

"Yaaaaaggghhhh!" she screamed.

The noise of her voice and the guitar was so loud that it was as if a great gale was buffeting the audience from the stage.

"No!" shouted Cy Smoothe, but it was too late. Something black flew off his head. Only when Ms Wiz stopped singing and screaming and the wind died down, did it become clear what had happened.

Cy Smoothe was sitting in his chair. His head was as bald and shiny as a billiard ball.

"Cut! He screamed, trying to cover his head with his hands. "Cut!"

"What happened, Mother?" Back home, Mr and Mrs Harris sat staring at a blank television screen.

"I rather think Ms Wiz lost her temper," said Mrs Harris. "And Cy Smoothe lost his hair. I never knew he wore a wig."

"Never mind that," said Mr Harris. "What about the Groovy Butterflies of whatsit?"

Just then the picture on the TV screen flickered into life. It showed two pandas sitting in a tree, eating bamboo shoots.

"We seem to be having technical problems with *I'm Talented, Make Me a Star!*," said the voice of an announcer. "So, instead of this week's programme, here's a really nice documentary about Giant Pandas."

"Pandas, Mother?" Mr Harris stared about him wildly. "Pandas in a talent competition? That can't be right."

"The show's off, Cuthbert," said Mrs Harris.

"But . . . what about my £100,000?"

Mrs Harris sighed. "It's exactly as you said, Cuthbert." She laid her hand on his. "About guitars. I'm afraid there's been a bit of unnecessariness."

When all the acts on *I'm Talented, Make Me a Star!* discovered that their show had been replaced by a documentary about pandas, there was confusion backstage at the Cy Smoothe Television Theatre.

Millie Piper the Little Nightingale was having a tantrum. Her mother was shouting into a mobile telephone. Billy from Absolutely Barking had bitten Harry "Mr Piano" Brown on the leg. The Hey Babes were not speaking to one another for reasons that no one could quite understand.

Podge, Jack and Ms Wiz had been taken to an office at the back of the theatre.

"I think you've caused quite enough trouble for one night," Trudi told them as she left them there. "I shall inform you when a car is ready to take you all home." She closed the door firmly behind her.

"Nice one, Ms Wiz," said Jack. "You've really done it now."

"Yeah," said Podge. "So much for giving peace a chance."

Ms Wiz had slumped into a chair behind the desk and sat, one leg hooked over the arm of the chair. She picked moodily at her electric guitar.

"Nobody calls Ms Wiz an old hippy," she said. "But *nobody*."

"It was an incredible guitar solo," said Podge. "I wish I could play like that."

Ms Wiz smiled. "You will one day,"

she said. "Start with the ukulele. The solos will come later."

At that moment, the door opened, It was Cy Smoothe. His smile was back in place, and so was his hair. In his hand was a sheet of paper and a pen.

"You destroyed my show." He spoke quietly. "You made me look very silly on live TV. The Groovy Butterflies are finished on this show."

"You said the boys were good," said Ms Wiz.

Cy Smoothe gave a little laugh. "They're OK but I've decided that the other kid – Millie, the Little Nightingale – is going to win this week. Maybe they can try again next year."

"I thought it was the viewers who decided who wins," said Podge.

Cy waved him aside. He approached the desk where Ms Wiz was sitting. "But I've never heard anyone play the guitar like that." He smiled toothily at

Ms Wiz. "You were incredible out there, babe."

"I am not your babe," said Ms Wiz coldly.

"Tell you what," said Cy Smoothe. "If you agree to let me be your manager, I can make you a rock goddess."

Ms Wiz shrugged. "A rock goddess? Me?"

"You'll be an international superstar," said Cy. "Playing all round the world. You'll have your own private jet."

"I would rather like a private jet," said Ms Wiz quietly. "It's what I've always wanted. I wouldn't mind being an international superstar, come to think of it."

Podge cleared his throat, then turned to Jack. "What was that about magic and selfish purposes Ms Wiz once told us?" he asked.

"Oh yes," said Jack. "Something about a golden rule, wasn't it?"

"Shut up, boys," snapped Cy Smoothe. "It's grown-up time." He laid the sheet of paper in front of Ms Wiz and held out a pen. "This is a record contract," he said softly. "It will make you rich and famous. All you have to do is sign."

Ms Wiz took the pen, looked at it, then laid it on the desk. She reached into her bag and took out her pink mobile phone. "I need to talk to my people," she said.

"Your people?" Cy Smoothe looked alarmed. "Who are your people?"

Smiling at Podge and Jack, Ms Wiz pressed "Redial". A low humming noise began to fill the room.

"See you, rock goddess," said Podge.

She gave a little wave as she began to vanish.

"What's happening?" said Cy Smoothe. "Where's she going? Stop . . . vanishing like that! I can make you a star!"

With a final little 'pop', Ms Wiz and her electric guitar disappeared.

Cy Smoothe turned to Podge and Jack. "OK, kids. Before we order you a taxi, I think you should tell me what's going on here."

"Ms Wiz has left the building," said Jack, like an announcer. "Ms Wiz has left the building."

There was silence in the office for a moment.

Podge held up his ukulele. "Who'd like a song?" he asked.

YOU'RE NICKED,
Ms Wiz

CHAPTER ONE
A SORT OF MISSING PERSON

"Daydreaming *again*, Lizzie Thompson?"

The words came to Lizzie from far away. She had been staring out of the window into the playground at St Barnabas School, unaware that her class teacher Mr Bailey was standing in front of her desk.

"Sorry, sir," she said quietly. "I was thinking about my cat."

"Your what?"

"My cat. Waif."

"Oh I see," said Mr Bailey. "Here we all are in the middle of an English lesson, discussing similes, and Lizzie's off in a private fantasy about her cat. That's absolutely fine then, isn't it?"

"It's lost, sir," said Jack, who was one of Lizzie's best friends. "It disappeared yesterday."

"Well, staring out of the window's not going to help, is it?" said the teacher briskly.

"Cruel," muttered Podge at the back of the class. "How would he like it?"

Mr Bailey thumped Lizzie's desk. "I would like it if Class Five did some *work* for a change," he said loudly. "Now, back to similes. Here is an example of a simile: 'Podge sits at his desk like a sack of potatoes.' Now who can give me another simile?"

Caroline put up her hand.

"Our teacher is like someone who doesn't know how you feel when you lose a pet and then he can't even manage to be nice when a person's so upset that she can't concentrate on a boring English lesson, especially when it's taught by a cat-hater. Or is that a metaphor, sir?"

Everybody in Class Five laughed – except for Lizzie, who was looking out of the window again.

After school, Lizzie ran home, hoping for the best but fearing the worst. All day, she had been unable to think of anything but Waif. Now, as she ran, she remembered the winter's day when she had found him, cold, shivering and hungry, among the dustbins by her house. He had hardly been more than a kitten. When no one came to feed him after a few days, she took him in. "Waif" she had called him.

And now he was gone.

"I've looked everywhere," said Lizzie's mother, when she arrived home. "In cupboards. Down the street. In the park—" she hesitated. "Under cars."

Tears welled up in Lizzie's eyes.

"You think he's dead, don't you?" she said.

Mrs Thompson put her arm around her daughter. "It's dangerous for cats around here. People drive so fast," she said, adding gently, "He's had a good innings."

"He's only six, Mummy," sobbed Lizzie. "Since when has six been a good innings?"

She ran upstairs to her room and slammed the door.

The next morning, Lizzie did something she had never done before. After waving goodbye to her mother at the end of her street, she walked towards St Barnabas as usual but, instead of turning right towards the High Street where she normally met Jack and Caroline, she turned left into the park.

"I just know that Waif is alive," she muttered to herself, "and today I'm going to find him."

"Good for you, dear," said an old tramp woman who was sitting on a park bench nearby, but Lizzie was too deep in thought to pay her any attention.

Lizzie's plan to find Waif went like this:

1. Look under a lot of bushes.
2. Pin up on trees the notices she had written late last night. They read: "LOST: BEAUTIFUL WHITE CAT WITH GINGER PATCHES (MALE). ANSWERS TO NAME OF WAIF (OR WAIFY). MUCH LOVED. IF FOUND, PLEASE PHONE 579 8282."

3. Go to the police station and ask for their help.

But nothing went right. All morning, Lizzie looked under bushes without success. She pinned up her notices, but then there were so many other lost cat notices that she began to despair.

"Everyone round here seems to have lost a cat recently," she sighed.

Finally, late that afternoon, she stumbled into the local police station.

"And what can I do for you, young lady?" asked the police constable behind the desk.

"I've lost my cat," said Lizzie nervously.

The policeman chuckled, as if he'd just been told a rather good joke.

"D'you know what this is, young lady?" he said, tapping a big book in front of him. "It's called the Crime

Book. In this book, I note down all the really terrible things that people get up to in this area. Theft, hit and run, breaking and entering, bag-snatching, vagrancy, motor offences, missing persons, grievous bodily harm – all sorts of nastiness."

"I see," said Lizzie.

"And now you want me to add to the list of ongoing, unsolved misdemeanours one little moggie that's gone walkabout, right?"

"He's a sort of missing person, too."

"Listen, miss. I know cats. They wander. Especially toms."

"He's not a tom," said Lizzie. "He's . . . neuter."

The policeman looked confused. "New to what?" he asked. "If he's new to the area, no wonder he's lost."

"PC Boote." Another policeman,

who had overheard the conversation,
now joined them. He winked at
Lizzie. "When the young lady says
her cat's neuter, I think she means
that he's—" He whispered into the
police constable's ear.

"Oh dear, oh dear," said PC Boote,
wincing slightly. He turned to Lizzie.
"When did this, er, neutering happen
then?"

"Don't worry, miss," said the

second policeman quickly. "We'll let you know if we hear of a lost cat. Just give PC Boote here the details."

Sighing heavily, PC Boote noted in the Crime Book Lizzie's name, telephone number and her description of Waif.

"Looking for lost cats," he muttered. "I've heard it all now."

Lizzie turned to leave. Somehow finding Waif was turning out to be even more difficult than she thought it was going to be.

Miserably, she stood on the steps of the police station, wondering what to do next.

"What you need is a spot of magic," said a familiar voice. It was the tramp who had seen Lizzie in the park. She was pushing a pram full of old rags, on which sat a china cat with odd, glowing eyes.

"Thanks," sniffed Lizzie. "And

where exactly do you find magic these days?"

"Follow me," said the tramp.

CHAPTER TWO
A STRANGE COINCIDENCE

Mr Bailey was panicking.

Yesterday, Lizzie Thompson had been upset about her cat. And what had he done? He had shouted, told her to get on with her work and hit the desk with his hand. And now Lizzie was absent from class. He had gone too far yet again. He would just have to ask the head teacher to ring her mother.

Mrs Thompson was panicking.

When the head teacher had rung to find out whether Lizzie was ill, she had been at work. It was three in the afternoon before she found out that her daughter had been missing all day. Then she rang the police.

PC Boote was panicking.

As soon as the report of a missing girl came through, he realised that this was the very same girl he had seen that afternoon.

"And what happened to her, police constable?" asked the station sergeant.

"She walked out of the station, sarge," mumbled PC Boote.

"And?"

"Er, I think I might have seen her walking off with a tramp."

The police sergeant sighed and reached for a telephone. This could be serious – very serious indeed.

"But I don't understand why you're all dressed in rags, Ms Wiz."

Lizzie and the tramp woman were sitting in a dingy café, drinking tea. Outside, it was already getting dark. An old man at the next table was darting suspicious looks in their direction as he shook a tomato ketchup bottle over his egg and chips.

"The last time I saw you," Lizzie continued, "you were a teacher."

Ms Wiz smiled.

"Do you remember what I told you then?" she asked. "I said I'd be back whenever a spot of magic was needed. So here I am."

"I see," said Lizzie quietly. She was beginning to wonder whether she was right to be here, sitting in a café with Ms Wiz. A worrying thought had occurred to her. Maybe it was somebody *pretending* to be Ms Wiz. What if this was the Danger Stranger she had always been told never to talk to?

"Watch," said the tramp woman, as if she could read Lizzie's mind.

There was a low hum from where she was sitting.

"Blimey!" said the man sitting at

the next-door table as the contents of
the tomato ketchup bottle covered
his plate.

"That's not magic," said Lizzie.
"That's life."

There was a slurping noise as the
ketchup disappeared back into the
bottle.

"*Blimey!*" gasped the man.

"Ms Wiz!" said Lizzie, laughing for
the first time that day. "You never
change, do you?"

"Only in the way I look," said Ms Wiz, taking a notebook from her pocket. "Now let's get down to business."

"D'you want a pen?" asked Lizzie.

"That won't be necessary," said Ms Wiz. "Cat's name?"

"Waif."

"Missing for how long?"

"Two days."

"Distinguishing features?"

"Green eyes, lovely white coat with

ginger patches . . ." Lizzie sighed as she remembered Waif. "Very friendly."

"Other facts known?"

"Only that everyone round here seems to have lost a cat."

"Mmm." Ms Wiz looked thoughtful. "Seems a strange coincidence."

"Yes," said Lizzie. "It is strange and all the lost cat notices mentioned that they had nice coats. That seemed a bit odd."

"Odd," said Ms Wiz, "and worrying. It's time for us to get moving."

"Aren't you going to note anything down?" asked Lizzie.

"Whoops, silly me," said Ms Wiz, staring hard at the notebook. As if an invisible hand were writing, the page quickly filled up with notes. "There you go," she said briskly.

Lizzie shook her head. Nothing was ever straightforward when Ms Wiz was around. "Now what do we do?" she asked.

"I'm going to tell you our plan," said Ms Wiz. "But before that, we're going to write to your mother, who'll be worrying about you. Then we're going home."

"To *your* home?" Lizzie couldn't believe her ears. When she was a teacher, Ms Wiz had always been very mysterious about where she lived and no one from Class Five had been invited back.

"It's not much," shrugged Ms Wiz, "but I think you'll like it."

It was dark by the time a letter from Lizzie was slipped under Mrs Thompson's door.

It read:

Dear Mum

Please don't worry about me. I'm alright and I've met up with someone who's going to use magic to help me find Waif.

Do you remember Ms Wiz our magical teacher? People called her a witch but she always said that she was a Paranormal operative. Well, it's her. Except now she's a tramp.

I'm staying at Ms Wiz's home, so everything is alright.

Love

Lizzie
xxx

PS Don't get the police to look for us. They probably wouldn't recognize me since Ms Wiz's plan is to turn me into a cat!!!

Mrs Thompson read the note again. Slowly the awful truth began to sink in.

Her only daughter had run off with a tramp . . .

Or maybe a witch . . .

And she was about to be turned into a cat . . .!

With a little cry, Mrs Thompson ran to telephone the police.

CHAPTER THREE
MAGIC – OR TROUBLE?

"Is this it?"

Lizzie was unable to keep the disappointment from her voice when they reached Ms Wiz's home.

Because it wasn't really a home at all. It was an extremely old car with flat tyres and dents all over it. It did have curtains but even they were more like rags, hung over the windows to stop people peering in.

"Yes, this is it," said Ms Wiz proudly. "What d'you think?"

"Interesting," said Lizzie, who didn't want to hurt Ms Wiz's feelings. "Not quite what I expected but . . . interesting."

"If you like it now, just wait until you step inside."

Ms Wiz opened the door with a flourish. Lizzie gasped.

From the outside, Ms Wiz's car had looked no more than a tangle of rusty, useless metal, just the sort of place where you might expect a tramp to live, but inside . . .

. . . it was even worse. All that Lizzie could see were torn, grey rugs, old newspapers and half-eaten sandwiches. Then something moved on the back seat – something small and grey.

"A rat!" Lizzie screamed.

"Of course," said Ms Wiz. "Don't you remember Herbert, my magic rat?"

She picked up Herbert and clambered into the car. "You can use the guest bedroom," she said, pointing to the back seat. Reluctantly, Lizzie climbed in.

"Close the door behind you," said Ms Wiz.

Something very strange happened as Lizzie pulled the door shut. There was a low hum and, as if someone had thrown a switch somewhere, the car started changing. The front seats turned around and became small armchairs. A table with crisps and lemonade appeared out of the floor. The back seat became a sofa. And the gearstick was transformed into a lamp which lit up the inside of the car with a soft pink glow.

Lizzie couldn't believe her eyes. It was as if she was no longer in a rusty old wreck of a car but in a warm country cottage.

"Being a Paranormal Operative has its advantages," smiled Ms Wiz.

"What are we going to do now?" asked Lizzie, settling down on the sofa. She was beginning to feel sleepy.

"We'll wait up for the catnappers," said Ms Wiz.

"Catnappers?"

"That's where your Waif has gone," said Ms Wiz. "And those other cats. They've been kidnapped, I'm sure of it."

"But why?"

"Gloves," said Ms Wiz grimly. "Fur gloves. That's why all the cats that have disappeared have nice coats."

Suddenly Lizzie felt afraid. Looking under bushes was one thing. But staying up all night to catch a

gang of catnappers? For a moment, she wished she was back in her bed, safe.

"Help yourself to crisps," said Ms Wiz, peering through the curtains into the darkness of the park outside. "I'll keep look-out. All the local cats come to this park at night and I have a feeling that our friends the catnappers will be here too. They'll lead us to Waif."

"How do you know he's alive?" Lizzie asked.

"Let's just put it down to intuition," said Ms Wiz.

Lizzie felt braver now. After all, she was with Ms Wiz. They had magic on their side.

"Jack, a policeman's here to ask you some questions."

Jack Beddows had just been dozing off when his mother switched on the light. There, in his bedroom, stood a policeman with a notebook in his hand.

"Sorry to interrupt your beauty sleep, young man," said PC Boote, "but we have a small emergency concerning your friend Lizzie."

Jack rubbed his eyes. "What's happened to her?" he asked.

"Her mother has received a letter

which gives us reason to believe
that she has been abducted by a
certain—" PC Boote looked in his
notebook "—Ms Wiz."

"Ms Wiz!" Jack sat up in his bed.
"Where is she?"

"That's the problem," said PC
Boote. "At first we thought she was
just a tramp but now it turns out that
she's an all-round troublemaker. We
think Lizzie's gone off with her."

"That's all right then," said Jack.

"All right?" PC Boote seemed surprised. "According to information received, this Ms Wiz has in the past turned teachers into geese, removed a school inspector's trousers and released about a thousand white mice into the children's ward of a general hospital. That's not what I call all right."

"Ms Wiz is magic," said Jack.

PC Boote put on his most serious expression. "You call it magic, son," he said. "I call it trouble. Now, we need to know exactly what she looks like.

"Here we go," said Ms Wiz, peering through the curtains of her car.

A van drew up by the gates of the park. Two men in dark clothes stepped out and climbed over the railings. The younger and taller of the two men was carrying a net while the other, a short, elderly man with a slight limp, followed him, whistling softly.

"Come on then," whispered Ms Wiz, shaking Lizzie by the shoulder.

"Mmmm?" said Lizzie sleepily.

"Our friends are here," said Ms Wiz. "It's time to put our plan into action."

After no more than half an hour, the men returned. They were carrying two cats, trapped in the net.

"This tabby puss is a young 'un," said the older man. "Shall I let it go?"

"Young or old, makes no difference," said the other man, opening the back of the van and bundling the cats into a sack. "And stop calling them 'puss'. Sometimes I think you're too soft for this game."

"What do we do now?" Lizzie

whispered as, moments later, the van
began to move.

"Follow them, of course,"
answered Ms Wiz. "Just because my
home's got four flat tyres, it doesn't
mean it can't go."

And, sure enough, the old car
seemed to raise itself slightly at that
moment and, as if hovering just above
the ground, moved quietly forward
to follow the van.

"The moment we arrive, we put our plan into action," said Ms Wiz as they drove quietly down the dark streets, always keeping a safe distance from the catnappers in front of them.

"Right," said Lizzie quietly. She was thinking of her mother, and how worried she would be. Still, there was no going back now.

Ms Wiz glanced over her shoulder.

"Nervous?" she asked.

"Not really," Lizzie lied. "So long as you're there to help."

Soon the van drew up outside a large dark house with closed shutters.

"I know this place," whispered Lizzie. "It's called the Old Hospital."

"All right," said Ms Wiz, stopping the car. "Ready?"

The men were getting out and opening the back of the van.

"Ready," said Lizzie, closing her eyes.

There was a low hum from the front of the car. Lizzie felt as if she had been slapped hard on the back. When she opened her eyes, everything in the car was bigger. She was looking up at Ms Wiz, who was smiling.

"What a lovely cat," Ms Wiz said. "Now remember the plan. You follow

them into the house and, as soon as
you're alone with the cats, scratch
your left ear three times. I'll be outside
and, as soon as I get that message,
I'll turn you back into Lizzie again.
Then you let the cats out, all right?"

"Sure," said Lizzie with a cat smile.
To her surprise, she found that she
could still talk in her normal voice.

The men were carrying the sack up
the steps to the house when Lizzie,
now a sleek black cat, went after them.

As they opened the door, she slipped in behind them.

Ms Wiz stood by her car, staring up at the house. "Good luck, Lizzie," she muttered.

It was then that she felt a heavy hand on her shoulder.

"You're nicked, Ms Wiz," said PC Boote.

CHAPTER FOUR
ABANDONED

It wasn't bad being a cat, Lizzie discovered.

Nobody noticed you, for example. You could creep under tables and hide in the shadows. You could jump onto window-ledges, as if it were the most natural thing in the world. And, even if you did lose your balance, you always seemed to land on your feet. It was quite fun.

Or at least it would have been if Lizzie had been in a normal house rather than in a catnappers' den.

Lizzie quickly discovered where they kept the cats. The older of the catnappers had trudged down to the cellar with the sack on his back. There was an unearthly yowling sound as a door was opened.

"There you go, my lovelies," he said. "Good puss." Lizzie heard hissing and scrabbling as the two new cats were bundled into the room. She ducked under a chair as the man returned, carrying an empty sack.

"That's about it then," he said to the other catnapper. "Mrs D'Arcy from the fur shop will be along tomorrow morning to tell us which ones she needs. Then," – for a moment he looked almost sad – "it's bye-bye, pussies."

"This is the last time I take you on a job," said the younger man. "Honestly, a catnapper that likes cats! I've heard it all now."

The older man sniffed. "I feel sorry for them, that's all. You wouldn't understand."

"If you like them so much, you'd better feed them."

The man fetched a paper sack of cat food and calling out, "Din-dins, pussies," he limped down the stairs. Lizzie followed.

For a moment, as he opened the door and threw some food in, there was total confusion in the room – and, in that moment, Lizzie slipped in.

What she saw took her breath away.

There were cats everywhere. Some were fighting over the food, some were miaowing pitifully, some were pacing backwards and forwards, some were simply asleep. One or two of the cats, startled to hear a human voice coming from a cat, arched their backs and hissed nervously.

"Don't worry," said Lizzie, carefully stepping through the throng of cats. "I'm just looking for someone. I'm not really a cat myself."

At that moment, a big ginger tom stepped forward and cuffed her around the ear.

"Ow!" said Lizzie. Without thinking she tapped him back, leaving her claws out. Surprised, the tom retreated backwards into a tabby, which bit him.

"Stop fighting, you stupid animals," said Lizzie angrily. "Don't you realise that tomorrow you could be . . ." At that moment, Lizzie saw a familiar white form in a corner. "Waif?"

The white cat stirred, recognising the voice, and gave a soft miaow. Lizzie looked closer. Yes it *was* Waif – asleep as usual.

It was time for action. Soon the catnappers would be going to bed. All Lizzie needed to do was to give Ms Wiz the signal to turn her back into a human, sneak out of the door, and then lead the cats to freedom.

Bracing herself for the shock, Lizzie scratched herself three times behind the left ear.

Nothing happened.

"Come on, Ms Wiz," she muttered, trying to keep calm. "Get that magic working." She scratched again, harder this time.

But nothing happened.

"Ms Wiz, where *are* you?" With growing desperation, Lizzie scratched and scratched and scratched.

But absolutely nothing happened.

"Don't you understand? Magic doesn't work at long distance. I can't change Lizzie back into a little girl from here."

Ms Wiz was sitting in a small, white-walled room at the police station. For the past hour, she had been trying to explain to PC Boote exactly why she needed to return to the catnappers' house as soon as possible.

"I see," said the police constable. "So your, er, magic is a bit like my walkie-talkie, is it? You have to be in range for it to work."

Ms Wiz sighed wearily. Why was it that grown-ups found it so difficult to understand magic when children found it so easy?

"That's right," she said.

"And you expect me to believe that you've cast a spell—" PC Boote could hardly keep the disbelief out of his voice "—transforming Lizzie Thompson into a cat in order to save a load of moggies from a couple of nasty men who want to turn them into gloves. And that's why you were at the Old Hospital."

"Precisely," said Ms Wiz.

"You must think I'm daft."

119

Ms Wiz was about to reply when the door opened. It was the station sergeant.

"Any luck, constable?" he asked.

"I'm afraid not," said PC Boote. "We're still in the land of witches and wizards."

"Right," said the sergeant. "She can spend the night in the cells. Tomorrow morning we've got two of Lizzie's classmates coming in to tell us whether this really is the famous Ms Wiz."

"You don't seem to understand," said Ms Wiz. "Tomorrow could be too late."

PC Boote turned to the sergeant and, with a grim little smile, tapped the side of his head.

At first, when they were led into the small room at the police station, Jack

and Caroline didn't recognise Ms Wiz. After a worried, sleepless night in the cells, she looked more like a tired, dishevelled tramp than ever.

Then she smiled.

"Ms Wiz!" said Caroline, hugging her.

"You look so different," said Jack.

"Hullo, Caroline and Jack," said Ms Wiz. "Could you explain to this policeman who I am?"

But, as the children told PC Boote about Ms Wiz, he continued to look suspicious.

"I'll need to discuss this with my superiors," he said eventually.

"There's no time for that," said Ms Wiz angrily. She turned to the children. "Do either of you know the way to the Old Hospital?"

"I do," said Jack.

Suddenly the sound of a low hum

filled the room. PC Boote was just about to speak when something very odd happened. He turned into a white rabbit.

"Sorry about that," said Ms Wiz, unlocking the door to the room with the keys that were now on the floor. "Let's go, children."

The police station now appeared to be completely empty, except for a number of white rabbits.

"Did you have to turn the whole police force into rabbits?" asked Jack as they hurried out of the main entrance. "There's going to be terrible trouble."

"I couldn't mess around," said Ms Wiz briskly. "This is a matter of life and death."

"Why didn't you do it earlier then?" asked Caroline.

"I didn't know the way to the Old Hospital," said Ms Wiz. "I may be magic but my sense of direction is terrible."

Outside the station stood a police car. Ms Wiz opened the car door and, pushing a white rabbit aside, leapt into the driver's seat.

"Jump in!" she shouted. The police car's engine started with a roar. "Let's just hope we're in time."

CHAPTER FIVE
FUR FREE

A thin ray of light penetrated the gloom of the cellar at the Old Hospital. Lizzie lay dozing, curled up beside Waif. Her left ear was sore from where she had been scratching all night. She was frightened.

Some of the cats around her stirred restlessly as they heard the sound of footsteps approaching the cellar. The door was flung open to reveal the most extraordinary woman Lizzie had ever seen. She was very tall and was wearing fur from head to foot.

"Ugh, disgusting!" said the woman. "If there's one thing I hate, it's live creatures."

"Think of them as pelts, Mrs D'Arcy," said the younger catnapper

nervously. "That's what they will be soon."

Mrs D'Arcy looked around the room.

"Frankly," she said, "there are some pelts here that I wouldn't allow my chauffeur to clean my car with."

The older man looked shocked. "Madam uses fur on her car?" he asked.

"I use fur for everything," said Mrs D'Arcy with a dangerous smile.

"Every item of clothing that I wear was once alive." She stroked her soft mink coat. "Now – let's get down to business. Count these horrible animals and I'll tell you how much I can pay."

The police car arrived at the Old Hospital with a squeal of brakes.

"Look, Ms Wiz!" said Jack, pointing to a large grey Rolls Royce, with a number plate which read "FUR 1", which was parked outside the front door.

"Just as I feared," said Ms Wiz, jumping out. "The fur merchant is here. Come on!"

Jack and Caroline followed her up the steps. Without hesitating, Ms Wiz kicked the front door, causing it to open with a loud crack.

"Wow," said Caroline. "Magic!"

"No," said Ms Wiz grimly. "That wasn't magic. That was anger."

Just then the older catnapper limped up the stairs from the cellar.

" 'Ere, what are you lot doing?" he said.

"We're here for the cats, so don't try and stop us," said Ms Wiz.

The old man smiled. "Stop you rescuing my little pussies? Why would I do that?" He winked as he walked past them towards the door. "I'll leave you to it. Good luck."

"Was *that* magic?" asked Jack.

"No, I think it was something called conscience," replied Ms Wiz.

At that moment, the three of them became aware of someone else climbing the stairs towards them.

"I don't know who you are," said a loud voice from the darkness in front of them. "But my name is Mrs D'Arcy. I'm very rich, very powerful and, when I'm annoyed, I can be very unpleasant."

"Careful, Ms Wiz," whispered Jack. "She looks as if she means it."

"We want those cats," Ms Wiz called out. "Open that door right now."

Mrs D'Arcy laughed. "I'm sure you do," she said. "From the way you're dressed, you look as if you could use a fur coat."

"I'm fur free," said Ms Wiz, moving closer.

"That's quite far enough," warned Mrs D'Arcy. "You're probably absolutely filthy. I don't want any nasty marks on my fur coat."

"What fur coat?" asked Ms Wiz innocently, as the sound of a low hum filled the basement stairs.

Automatically, Mrs D'Arcy touched her coat – and gasped. The fur was beginning to move, as if it had a life of its own.

"What's happening?" she said, going pale.

"Nothing much," said Ms Wiz. "I'll release the cats in a moment. But first of all, I want to free the animals that made your coat."

Before Jack's and Caroline's astonished eyes, Mrs D'Arcy's clothes were becoming a writhing mass of animals.

"But everything I'm wearing is fur," she shrieked.

"Oh dear," said Ms Wiz. "How very embarrassing."

By now, Mrs D'Arcy's coat had completely disappeared and several small, furry animals were shaking and scratching themselves at her feet. With a scream, she ran up the stairs, as the rest of her clothes began to turn back into animals.

Ms Wiz opened the door to the cellar. The second of the two catnappers was standing, apparently unable to move, in the middle of the room. One of the cats had gone to sleep on his feet.

"I thought of turning him into a mouse," said Ms Wiz. "But in the end I decided on a human statue. Cats can be so cruel."

"There's Waif!" shouted Caroline, pointing across the room.

"Never mind Waif," said Jack. "What about Lizzie?"

At that moment, a sleek black cat stretched sleepily and scratched herself three times behind the left ear.

"Lizzie!"

Within moments of becoming a human being again, Lizzie had telephoned her mother. Now, minutes

later, mother and daughter were
hugging each other joyfully on the
steps of the Old Hospital.

"Where's Waif?" asked Mrs
Thompson.

"He's being fed in the kitchen with
the other cats," said Jack. "We're
going to hold on to them until we can
find all their owners."

"And who on earth is that odd
woman hiding in the Rolls Royce
without any clothes on?"

Lizzie laughed. "It's a long
story," she said. "Perhaps Ms Wiz had
better explain it. Where is she, by the
way?"

"Oh no!" said Jack, who had
noticed Ms Wiz's battered old car
rising slowly off its flat tyres like a
hovercraft about to move off. "She
can't go now."

A white rabbit was hopping busily
down the road towards them.

"Ms Wiz!" shouted Lizzie. "You've forgotten the police! They're still rabbits!"

The car hesitated and hovered with a low hum.

"All right," said PC Boote, shaking himself as if he had just awoken from a rather strange dream. "Where are these catnappers then?"

"The ringleader's over there," said Lizzie, pointing to Mrs D'Arcy's car. "But she's—"

"No buts," said the policeman. "Leave this to me."

He walked slowly towards the Rolls Royce.

"Right, you in there," he said, bending down to look in the window. "You're nicked. Er, you're nacked. Oh no, you're absolutely n-n-n-naked!"

He turned away, blushing.

And everyone, even PC Boote, started laughing.